THE HIGHWAY
Every Life Counts

PRASHANT PATHAK

INDIA • SINGAPORE • MALAYSIA

ISBN 979-8-88749-316-9

I dedicate this Novel to my Elder Brother Advocate Santosh Pathak who believed me in every stage of life he was with in the journey of writing this book

PREFACE

I am publishing "The Highway" – a story that stays close to me after 7 years, where technology is taking over mankind. We, as humans, are losing the value of another human being. Talking on the phone while driving and riding has become the reason for many road accidents.

That one call can lead to the death of pedestrians. It can kill the driver and the people sitting inside the vehicles or make our life and body handicapped. At the end of the day, we only have regrets in our life to live with.

The highway is a story of Vijay who lost his family in such an accident. Not only does he survive to die internally every day but he finds the reason to relive on the highway.

It was a torrid afternoon of summer when Dr. Priti arrived at an old Tarabai government hospital. She had gazed at the horde and rushed towards the hospital which was located on the highway to Shahpur. There were few shops around it and an ambulance was parked outside the gate. People were waiting in the corridor to meet their loved ones, ward boys were running around and doctors were checking on thousands of patients, after all, it was a hospital. No one can expect a pleasant view from a place where people fight for their lives every moment.

Dr. Priti went inside the hospital and asked the ward boy, "Can you tell me which of these is Dr. Shekhar's room?"

The ward boy showed her to Dr. Shekhar's office. Priti was quite excited to meet Dr. Shekhar and could not wait to start her work. She greeted Dr. Shekhar, "Good afternoon, sir."

Dr. Shekhar welcomed her with a warm smile on his face. He was quite happy to see her. "Oh! Dr. Priti Sharma, how are you? Welcome to our hospital, I was waiting for you," he replied with a tranquil voice.

By looking at her pale skin and watery eyes, Dr. Shekhar advised her to take some rest as she seemed really tired after a long journey. He suggested they could meet the next day, but Dr. Priti was reluctant as she had a determination to start her work the moment she arrived at Tarabai hospital.

"No sir, I am perfectly fine and I would like to take charge today itself. You can tell me about the cases," Dr. Priti said with conviction.

Dr. Shekhar was mesmerized by her response. He praised Priti, "Well, we have got what we have heard. That's the spirit." He grabbed the files and started introducing her to patients.

The first case was about Raju, who was a malaria patient. Dr. Shekhar mentioned that Raju was from a nearby village and that he was being treated in their hospital. He introduced several other patients to Dr. Priti and now it was her responsibility to take care of them.

After having a good talk, both of them went to see a special patient. It was quite a disastrous case that any mind could handle.

It was Vijay Srivastava's case, a young man lying on the bed who lost his entire family in an accident.

Dr. Shekhar started briefing Priti about this patient's history.

"This special file is of a patient who has been in a coma for the past three months. The patient's name is Vijay Srivastav. His was an accident case. He was brought in wounded condition. He was bleeding and had a major skull injury. It was too much for the doctors to handle at that time."

The doctors were somehow able to save him with surgery and medications, but he went into a coma for a long time. During the accident, two women and a little girl were also brought to the hospital with him. The heart-wrenching part was all three of them were brought there in dead condition. The police started investigating and found that one of them was his mother, the other one was his wife, and sadly that child was his younger daughter.

This case was a big challenge for Dr. Priti as she was upset on hearing Vijay's case history and had a teary eye for a moment. She noticed that Vijay has grown long hair that has not been cut for several months, with his beard rolling down up to his chest.

Dr. Priti asked, "Is there no one from his family around here, someone who can take care of him?"

Dr. Shekhar gasped and said, "Yes, Deendayal Ji, his uncle, has been taking care of him for the last three months. He is here with the hope that, at some point or other, Vijay will get out of that bed."

Life is all about uncertainties. It's a shocking truth for any person to know that his whole family was destroyed over a night. The doctors were scared to understand the fact that even if Vijay comes to his senses, nobody can predict how he will respond to the situation. The chances of him surviving were quite less but not zero.

Doctors were unsure what would happen to him after he got up from that bed. Every doctor in that hospital was trying his best to save his life.

The next day Dr. Priti was having a regular check-up for Vijay and other patients,

She gave an injection to Vijay and went to her cabin. Priti started studying Vijay's case file the entire night. She was sleepy but she continued to finish the case study.

Vijay was in a coma. But a miracle happened and life gave him another chance. His entire life flashed before his eyes. He smiled cherishing the moments of his daughter's birthday, moments he spent with his wife, his wedding day, all the lazy hours he spent on his mother's lap, and then…the accident.

He suddenly opened his eyes and started gasping. The nurse who was cleaning his body noticed that something was wrong with him. She was frightened and started screaming at the top of her lungs.

Dr. Priti ran towards his ward with all the ward boys and they witnessed that Vijay had gotten up by himself and was walking outside his room. He suddenly fell and bumped his head. He started bleeding.

Dr. Priti shouted, "Rajesh and Shamu grab him. Take him inside the ward."

She was worried about Vijay. It was quite a surprise for the entire hospital as many of them lost hope that he would ever recover. She tried to convince Vijay and pulled him towards his ward. But Vijay was not listening to any of them. One of the ward boys dragged him to his room and helped him to lie down on the bed.

Priti was continuously telling Vijay, "Please lie down, you were in a coma for the last three months."

But Vijay was pushing other staff and wanted to go to his family. He was searching for them all around the place. Although Vijay had come to his senses that day, he was unable to walk. He was shivering and losing his balance at every step. Priti was no longer surprised by the frailties and weaknesses that lead Vijay to fall many times. She was sure that if he tried to walk again, he was going to injure himself.

Vijay was not allowing anybody to touch him. He did not listen to anyone and started screaming and shouting. He must have woken up the entire hospital with his wailing cry. He was in sorrow, pain, and extreme grief that anyone could possibly imagine.

Vijay started yelling, "Leave me, leave me alone, let me go."

Dr. Priti realized that this incident would turn into a nightmare if she did not control Vijay.

Priti insisted Rajesh get the big rope and tie him up. If we did not stop him, it would lead to serious issues.

The ward boys tied up Vijay with the rope and helped Priti to give him an injection. As soon as she injected the syringe, Vijay went back to sleep. Everybody sighed for a moment.

She observed that Vijay had injured his head and told the nurse to bring some ointment and bandages. Priti put the dressing on his head scars. While putting bandages on his head Priti noticed a few words written on his hands. She looked at them carefully and saw it was his wife's and daughter's name, "Priti and Anamika". She saw that and looked at Vijay.

The next morning, Dr. Priti went to Shekhar's office to tell him that Vijay has regained consciousness. She went inside the office with a frisson of excitement.

Dr. Priti uttered, "Good morning sir, Vijay Srivastava is out of the coma, he regained consciousness at 1 am last night."

Dr. Shekhar was astounded to hear this and got a little confused too. He could not believe his senses and went numb for a moment.

"I can't believe it. Priti! Do you know when I performed the first surgery, I did not believe that he would survive? After surgery, he went into a coma and I lost all hope."

Dr. Priti consoled him and told him that his hard work had paid off. His dedication towards Vijay and keeping him protected has resulted in a new life.

"Sir, when the nurse told me about Vijay, I immediately entered his room. I was shocked to see that he got up from his bed. He was walking," Priti replied.

She described the whole incident last night, how Vijay started screaming and fell hard on his head. Although it was glad news for both the doctors, they were more worried about the future consequences. They knew the worst was coming to Vijay's path as the truth unveils about his family.

Both of them walked into his room and decided to talk to him. They were thrilled but excited about this recent development in Vijay's case.

Vijay has regained consciousness. Shekhar saw that he was tied completely from head to toe. He was trying hard to untie the rope and looking far and wide.

Dr. Shekhar greeted, "Good morning Mr. Vijay How are you feeling?"

Vijay gazed at him and got lost in himself. He started babbling and murmuring for a while.

Dr. Shekhar asked the same question again and this time Vijay replied with a bewildered look on his face. Vijay raised his eyes towards him and asked, "Who are you guys? Where is my family?"

Dr. Shekhar introduced himself and Dr. Priti. He tried to calm him down by rubbing his back.

Vijay had a spark in his eyes the moment he heard the name Priti. It certainly reminded him of his beloved wife. But he was asking again the same question about his mother, wife, and daughter. And what happened to them? He was desperate to meet them.

Dr. Shekhar panicked and lied that they all were fine and went home yesterday. He diverted the topic and suggested Vijay meet his uncle.

Dr. Priti was confused after listening to Shekhar's response. She suddenly turned her head around and raised her eyebrows. She was not very happy with his reaction.

Vijay was surprised at how he ended up in this situation, tied up with rope and lying on the bed.

Dr. Priti tried to explain to him that it was necessary under circumstances. She told him last night he came to his senses after three months and started walking after getting up from his bed. He wasn't listening to anyone and fell. Vijay then realized that there was a bandage on his head.

Vijay was in dire need of rest, Dr. Priti pulled his bed sheet and told him to sleep. Dr. Shekhar realized that he had committed something serious to Vijay. He ran towards the corridor and started searching for his uncle, Deendayal.

After this Dr. Shekhar left Vijay's room Priti untied the ropes from Vijay's body. She was feeling sorry for Vijay but she was helpless in this situation.

Vijay suddenly opened his eyes and said, "Dr. Priti, your name reminds me of my wife and you can't even imagine how happy she would be, and my baby girl Anamika, she will go crazy after seeing me. It seems like I haven't heard her voice in eternity."

Dr. Priti had teary eyes and soon tears started rolling down her cheeks.

Vijay asked her, "Are you crying, Dr. Priti? What happened?" Priti quickly wiped her face and made an excuse. She told him to take a rest and rushed towards her office.

Dr. Shekhar saw Vijay's uncle sitting on the bench. Deendayal Ji, a poor old man was sobbing and watching all the people roaming around.

Shekhar gave this good news to Deendayal Ji. He told Deendayal that Vijay has regained consciousness, and he could meet him.

Deendayal Ji looked at the floor and started crying. He cried his eyes out for a few minutes.

Shekhar told him, "I know this is not a happy time for you, but you have to stay strong. You need to support Vijay. He has got a new life."

Deendayal Ji wiped his face. He was stunned and confused as to how to tell Vijay about his family.

He was wondering how Vijay would react when he comes to know there is no one else left in his world except him. His heart will be shattered into pieces.

25 Feb 2022

After all, he was like his child and Deendayal was worried about the consequences of that condition. There were thousands of questions bombarding his mind. How could he explain the situation to Vijay? What would he tell him about his daughter and wife? How would Vijay react?

He collapsed on the ground and thought that it would have been better if he too had died with them, he didn't have to face this dark patch of his life and sink into the sea of sorrow.

Dr. Shekhar helped him to get up and sat on the bench. Shekhar waited for a few minutes for Deendayal to calm down.

Shekhar was ashamed of his culpability in that situation but he had to ask Deendayal to be a part of his falsehood. He gathered the courage to ask Deendayal if he could lie to Vijay about the whole situation.

Deendayal was stunned by his response. He asked, "What? Why? How…how could you?"

Shekhar told him that Vijay was not in a condition where he could tell him the truth. That is why he lied and told him that his family is fine. He convinced him to tell the same.

The time was critical for Vijay as his health was not showing great positive signs. He could barely walk and eat. Under these circumstances, he would have got a shock and extreme depression after the revelation. There was a chance that a severe attack might have cost us his life. This time was very delicate for Vijay.

"Deendayal Ji, I hope you understand the situation", Shekhar asked with a gloomy tone.

Deendayal was not ready to be part of this lie. He couldn't hide the truth at this point.

He asked with a distraught face, "We can tell him this lie today but what will happen tomorrow? What would I do when he comes to know the truth? How do I deal with that?"

The time was testing everyone's courage and Deendayal was no exception. Telling his nephew that his family no longer exists in this world would be the last thing he could ever imagine in his life.

Dr. Shekhar assured Deendayal Ji that Vijay would be fine after a few months. They all could tell him the truth once his physical and emotional well-being marks all the checkpoints. But that present-day Vijay's condition was extremely bad to bear any truth.

Deendayal hesitated for a while but eventually agreed to Shekhar's suggestion. He believed that Vijay has got a new life and it was god' will to keep him alive. He understood that a patient's life does not remain the same after he gets out of a coma. Even a slight blow could have killed Vijay that day.

Both of them agreed to bury this truth inside their heart for a while and they decided to drink this bitter truth to save Vijay's life.

Deendayal Ji went to Vijay's room and pretended to laugh, hiding all his pain behind a smile.

Vijay got excited about his uncle. He was extremely happy.

He asked Deendayal Ji, "How are you, uncle? How is my mom? And Priti? Where is Anamika? Why didn't you bring them too?

Deendayal Ji told Vijay that they all were taking a rest at home. He made sure that Vijay believed they were all fine and was waiting for him to return home.

Vijay was delighted to know that and he was waiting to go home. He told his uncle that he desperately wanted to see Anamika. It was difficult for Vijay to live without them even for a moment.

Deendayal Ji was looking at Vijay and tears started rolling down his cheeks. His eyes were saying a lot of things that he could not speak through words. Vijay was surprised to see him crying,

He asked, "Why are you all crying since yesterday? Look now I'm fine. Is there something wrong with me?

Deendayal Ji wiped his tears and said, "No dear, these are tears of joy, you have dodged death. My brave boy! We are so happy for you."

Deendayal Ji and Dr. Shekhar went out to discuss the further procedure and when Vijay should be getting discharged. For the next few days, Deendayal Ji and other hospital staff took care of Vijay. They made him believe that everything was fine and he was going to go home soon.

One night before his discharge, Dr. Priti went into Vijay's room for a regular health check. She was thinking about the next day when Vijay is going to find out the truth. But she decided to avoid that thought and have a good conversation with Vijay before he leaves the hospital.

As soon as Dr. Priti entered his room, Vijay thanked her for saving his life.

Vijay looked at Dr. Priti with teary eyes. He said, "All this has been possible because of you guys. Dr. Shekhar and you are no less than god, my family would no longer be alive without you, I can never forget you both. Thank you!"

"If you need anything in your life, you must remember me. You can call me without any hesitation, anytime. I will be there to help you. I have given my address and number to Dr. Shekhar. After I go home, I will visit you with my family", he added.

Dr. Priti chuckled, her face as long as a fiddle indicating the grief behind her eyes. She told Vijay that no patient would return to see the doctor. But Vijay promised her that he would come to see her with his family.

Dr. Priti was curious to know about Vijay's life. She was surprised to see a man who loved his family so much.

She asked, "If you don't mind, can I ask you one thing? You love your family so much, what are they like? Why don't you tell me something about yourself? "

Vijay smiled and replied, "What do you want to know?"

Vijay had not told anyone about himself except his mother. He was quite a shy person.

He thought about it for a moment and realized that Dr. Priti deserved to know things about him. She was the one who saved his life.

Vijay started telling his story, "I am a software engineer in a Mumbai-based IT company. My mother always wanted me to become an engineer. She also wanted me to go abroad and have a successful life. I graduated and I started working so that I can get some experience. I had a plan to go abroad further. Mother took a lot of trouble with my studies, and she had a lot of expectations. Honestly, making her happy was the only goal of my life….until I met Priti, my wife."

A few years ago, Vijay was working for an IT company. It was a beautiful morning when Vijay was traveling to his office. He was carrying a laptop in his hand and got off the train. He then went to catch the rickshaw. That's when he saw a girl was also waiting for the rickshaw.

She was very beautiful, stubborn, a little arrogant, angry, and unbridled. People had to stand in a long queue for the sharing auto rickshaw. Vijay quickly ran to catch the line one day and the girl also came running from the other side.

They both came into the queue at the same time. Vijay was quite a gentleman so he stood behind her. The girl was standing in front of him and next to her was a fat little man. That man was on his phone and seemed very jolly.

Vijay saw Priti's hand. She was carrying bags that were too heavy. He asked Priti, "Let me lighten up your stuff. It seems quite heavy."

She rudely said, "No need for this kindness."

The fat little guy started laughing.

Vijay politely said, "Okay madam, I did the exact same thing last month. I was standing there with my luggage. One guy told me that he would like to lighten my stuff. I put my heavy bag in his hands. Looking back, he really did lighten my stuff and left."

The fat guy laughed his head off.

Priti murmured that this was supposed to happen with some stupid people. She was not a very happy-go-lucky girl.

Vijay heard her words and thanked her for praising him like that. The fat guy was overhearing the entire conversation and laughing continuously.

Then finally one auto-rickshaw arrived at the stand.

Vijay and the fat little guys got into that rickshaw. Both of them asked Priti to join them.

But usually, four people used to sit in a rickshaw, but this time only three people sat instead of four. Quite obvious, the fat little guy had occupied the two seats. So there was a small room left in that rickshaw for Priti.

Priti was not ready to go with them.

Vijay told her that getting a rickshaw takes hours in that area. She had to do her office work at the rickshaw stand if she didn't get into this one.

Priti said, "Shut up, you idiot."

But all the public started shouting, "Hey come on, if you don't want to go then step aside, other people are standing in the line. Let them go."

The rickshaw driver was also pissed with her behavior. He told her to get inside the rickshaw and sit or give the chance to someone else.

After creating a whole drama, Priti finally sat down with Vijay and the fat little guy.

Vijay was a fun-loving and happy-go-lucky guy. He made a few jokes and started making impressions on his way to the office. He made that fat guy laugh throughout their journey.

But Priti was irritated by hearing his chortle. She was completely pissed and angry.

She said, "Hey, fat ass. Why are you laughing? Shut up! If you laugh one more time I will break your jaw."

The fat guy was scared to death and remained silent in fear.

Vijay was not pleased with her reaction. He started criticizing her that no one can stop somebody from laughing in this free country. How could she have the guts to stop this free man's laughter?

Vijay told him, "You can laugh brother, nobody can stop you. I will see who can stop you."

Priti whispered, "I am not talking to you, I swear if he laughs one more time I will kick his ass."

Vijay made fun of her and forced that poor guy to laugh. He kept telling him not to worry about her but the poor fat guy was now stuck in this weird situation with both of them.

That guy finally decided to get out of that Rickshaw.

He shouted, "Hey boy, stop the rickshaw and let me get off. I don't know but these two are weird people and this lady might punch me."

A rickshaw was stopped near the gate. The poor fat man got off the rickshaw and ran away.

Vijay blamed Priti for her attitude. She spoiled all the fun that beautiful afternoon. She kept quiet and did not say a word.

The rickshaw finally reached her office and Priti got off towards the main gate.

Vijay tried to lighten up the mood while she was leaving and said, "He was a lovely man, but do you know why these fat people laugh so much? No, you can't tell. Because you are not fat."

Priti gazed at Vijay and ignored his blabbering.

He then told the rickshaw driver that Priti was getting late. He asked the driver to tell her the fare and carry on towards his destination.

The rickshaw driver replied, "Rs. 50 madam."

Priti got off the rickshaw and rushed to pay the fare. But Vijay told her not to pay anything. He was going to pay her fare.

He taunted her, "We do not allow any aunties to pay."

Priti shouted, "Did you call me Auntie?"

Vijay started laughing and told the driver to run. They both laughed saying that lady was super crazy.

While leaving the rickshaw, Vijay teased Priti by taking his head outside the rickshaw. He continued to laugh till he reached his office.

One day Vijay called the sharing rickshaw and Priti came out of nowhere, she went inside to grab the seat. Vijay was surprised but he tried to sit with her too, thinking that she might share the auto.

But when he went inside to sit, she got angry. She started saying that either Vijay will go in this rickshaw, or she will. She was always a hot-headed person.

Vijay was tired of her behavior so he let that go. Priti continued to argue that she had caught the rickshaw.

Vijay got pissed with her and both of them started fighting in the middle of the road. The auto driver got stuck in that situation. This used to happen almost every day.

The next day auto drivers started running away watching them fighting. Another day, Vijay had stopped the rickshaw but Priti repeatedly behaved the same way. Her actions made him really angry.

Vijay snapped at her, "O madam, I have stopped this rickshaw. How could you steal my auto?"

Priti arrogantly replied, "Hey Mr. Now that I have sat in the rickshaw, I will go. You can catch another rickshaw".

Vijay and Priti started fighting again. Every day they used to create a scene and people used to suffer from this drama.

Vijay was determined to teach her a lesson and quickly landed on an idea to do that. So the next day, Vijay kept waiting for Priti. He did not stand in the queue but simply stood in a corner. A few minutes later Priti arrived at the stand. As usual, she called for a rickshaw.

As soon as Priti had called for the rickshaw, Vijay ran towards her and sat in the rickshaw.

Then there was an everyday scene. Both of them started fighting again.

Priti was pissed, "Hey Mr. get down from the auto. I have called a rickshaw, and I will sit in it."

Vijay smiled and said, "Why madam? I stopped the rickshaw yesterday but you were very coercive during the fight. You got what you wanted. So today, I am just following in your footsteps.

I have given you the taste of your own medicine. How does it taste? But anyway I'm not as arrogant as you are. Come and sit here with me, I'll drop you."

Priti was disgusted by his behavior. She never had learned to hear NO from anyone and continued her arrogant behavior.

Vijay welcomed her politely and offered a seat in his rickshaw. He told her that she needed to calm down and stopped getting angry at small things.

Priti was still a stubborn and arrogant girl. She threatened him to complain to the police.

Vijay humorously said, "See you are suffering needlessly, I know you are a poor girl, I will not take money from you. I will give you the money.

Vijay told the driver to hurry up. Both of them started laughing at her behavior.

"Hey brother go, She seems to have flared up, speed up," said Vijay.

A week passed by and every day they both met at the same time, every time they fought for the same auto-rickshaw. Sometimes Vijay used to stop the rickshaw and Priti went to sit in that.

Sometimes Priti would stop the rickshaw, and then Vijay would repeat the same actions. It was an everyday drama for people around that stand. Every single person around that area was done with their fights. All the rickshaw drivers started avoiding them. They used to run away and hesitated to accept their ride.

One day Vijay came early to the rickshaw stand and went to a corner. He was hiding from Priti to see her reaction and stood there quietly. He was waiting for Priti to come.

After a few minutes, Priti reached the rickshaw stand. She started looking for Vijay. But Vijay saw her and remained silent. He was wondering what she was looking for.

Priti started searching for Vijay and asked people if they have seen him anywhere around the place. She adjusted her glasses and asked every person about Vijay. Her eyes told a lot about her feelings. She was unable to express herself and got confused. She was not sure what was happening to her. Vijay was sure that she was looking for him. He was watching her alone that day, she was desperately waiting for him. He felt something in his heart too but chose to remain quiet. All the rickshaw drivers were asking if she wanted a ride but she stayed like a statue. She did not leave the office that day and went home.

People were surprised. Every day she used to fight for the rickshaw. But that day she did not even bother to ask or stop any auto. How did this happen? Everyone was puzzled by her behavior.

After that incident, she used to reach the rickshaw stand and waited for Vijay. She used to wait for hours but every time got disappointed. For the last four days, she went home from that rickshaw stand. It was Vijay who made her feel alive, it was him who brought the rays of sunshine into her dark life. She was an introvert and could never express her feelings to anybody. Vijay continued to watch her for four days. The previous day, Vijay noticed that Priti had stopped taking care of herself. She was not doing any makeup, she had hardly tied up her hair and her skin looked pale.

The next day Vijay was standing on the front pavement and suddenly Priti's attention fell on him.

She kept looking at him but couldn't do anything.

She was watching him without a flinch. She stopped one rickshaw and sat in it. Vijay thought she left for the office but he was wrong. Vijay kept watching her until she left. But then he saw that the rickshaw went for a while and stopped at the signal. All the rickshaw drivers kept watching what was happening.

Priti was peeping out of the rickshaw and saw that Vijay was still standing there.

Priti screamed, "Stop driver… stop the rickshaw."

The rickshaw driver asked, "What's the matter, madam? Is something left behind? See there will be a traffic jam if we stop.

Priti smiled, "Perhaps, yes, something is left behind."

She got off the rickshaw and started looking towards Vijay. Vijay could not take his eyes off her. They were looking at each other in the middle of the road for five minutes. There was a huge traffic jam. Cars and autos were honking continuously. Priti took off her glasses and started crying.

It was a bit crowded but everyone kept looking at them. Priti ran towards Vijay and that was it! Vijay took Priti in his arms. Priti could not stop crying and all the rickshaw drivers started clapping.

Priti said that this idiot was so humble, that it became difficult for her to survive the entire week without him.

Vijay told her that he was aware of everything. She did not understand and asked him how he would know what was happening.

Vijay said, "I was watching silently what you have been doing for four days. Every day you went back home, I also noticed that you have stopped grooming. So much love was hidden in your heart. I cannot believe we used to fight every day. Can you at least tell me your name today?"

Priti answered with teary eyes, "My name is Priti… Priti Khanna and yours?"

Cars were honking and people were shouting in the middle of the road.

The public started complaining, "Hey brother, let the other people go, the government has made gardens for you guys."

Vijay and Priti started giggling. They apologized to all the people around there and started walking on the sidewalk. Both of them did not go to work that day.

Both were sitting in the garden.

Vijay asked Priti, "Why haven't you told me this? When did you fall in love with me?

Priti blushed and said, "I don't even know how it happened. From the day I waited for you at the rickshaw stand. I was scared and thought I missed something in life. I wanted to see your face. I don't know what happened that day. My feet were not supporting me, my brain stopped working and my mind was out of my control. I was only waiting for you all the time. I also thought of quitting my job. You didn't have any pity for me. You kept watching my situation. So cruel."

Vijay smiled and said, "I wanted to help you but I was curious to know how much you love me,

I wanted to see that yearning. I was amazed that such a hot-minded girl like you can also fall in love and to be honest, I fell in love with you too."

Someone has rightly said that love grows into three stages. First, they quarrelled, then agreed, and then fell in love. It happened because it was meant to happen. They kept meeting for several months. They were madly in love with each other.

One day Vijay took Priti to meet his mother. His mother was doing some work on the balcony when they reached home. Priti was all decked up, wearing a beautiful saree, golden earrings, and an elegant necklace.

Vijay asked, "Mother, someone has come to meet you."

The mother said that she was busy and he would go and check on that person.

Priti was confused, "What are you doing? I am with you, what is this?"

* * * * *

Vijay asked Priti to not say anything.

Vijay wished, "Shushushu Shush Uuuuuuuuuuuuuuuuuuuuuuuu, who are you? Whom do you want to meet? If you want to meet my mother, she is inside. You can tell me what you want…No? It's okay. I'll call mom, wait."

Priti got scared hearing this. She was confused as to why Vijay was doing this. She looked super panicked. Vijay was truly enjoying the whole scene.

Vijay called his mother. He told her that the guest in their house wanted to see her. Vijay's mother came outside the balcony, and she saw that a beautiful girl, all decked up, was wearing a saree. She was very impressed by Priti and her elegance.

Vijay's mother asked, "Who are you dear and why do you want to meet me?"

Vijay told his mother that he has no idea about this lady and purposely asked, "Hey, tell me why you want to meet my mother? Don't worry, you can tell her."

Priti was very nervous, she gazed at Vijay with a red face and told his mother that she came to visit her with Vijay but Vijay has gone mad. He was troubling Priti and smiling continuously.

Vijay pretended to be surprised, "With me? This girl is lying. Mother, I don't even know her.

Who are you? What's the matter with you? A lot is happening these days when someone sees a poor lady alone at home, they rob the house."

At that moment Priti got completely pissed and very upset with Vijay. She was scared but she could not stand him after hearing this.

Vijay's mother got to know that it was Vijay's usual trap. She asked Vijay to speak the truth.

But Vijay continued to lie and made Priti more nervous. He was checking poor Priti's patience at one point.

Priti snapped, "Okay. Fine. If you don't know me then I don't know you either. Goodbye."

Priti took her bag and started walking towards the door. Vijay realized that it was time to stop that drama. Vijay rushed towards her and stopped her. He started laughing out loud. But Priti was not very pleased with this joke. After all, she was a hot-headed person who fought with Vijay over the Auto Rickshaw.

Vijay held her hand and said sorry. He brought her inside the house and introduced her to his mother.

Vijay smiled and said, "Come here Priti, mom, this is Priti, I am so sorry I was just kidding, come on Priti. Don't be upset."

Vijay's mom started scolding him, "You are such a lunatic Vijay, you made this sweet girl cry. Sorry dear, it is his habit of kidding around like this. Welcome to our house"

Priti smiled and touched his mother's feet. His mom told Priti that Vijay has already revealed the secret about them. She already knew everything about Vijay and Priti since the day they started dating. She also said that Priti was the one who used to torture Vijay at the rickshaw stand but happened to fall in love with her son. But she was glad to see that both of them loved each other so much. Vijay's mother thanked God for sending such a beautiful and loving daughter-in-law to their house. She said, "I used to only worry that when I am not there, who will take care of this lunatic? But now that you are here, I am sure that you can take care of this crazy guy and also his stupid jokes, won't you? Honestly, I don't have much time left."

Vijay and Priti told his mom not to say anything like that. They promised her that they will take good care of her and remain a happy family till the end.

Vijay's mother embraced her kids and she started crying. She was extremely happy that day. She thought why God would have so much mercy on her. She suggested they get married soon and invited Priti for dinner the next weekend.

Vijay and Priti got married after six months. Vijay's mother always treated Priti as her own child. One year passed and then they had a beautiful daughter. Anamika was born on their second anniversary. It was the most precious day of Vijay's life. Anamika was the piece of his heart and his world would revolve around her. It was Anamika's third birthday when Vijay gifted her mouth organ. He wanted Anamika to have everything in this world that he could not get during his childhood.

He loved Priti and Anamika more than anything in this world. They were indeed a happy family.

By this time Dr. Priti started crying and continuously wiping her face. She was stunned to know that such a beautiful family has been destroyed due to someone's irresponsible behavior. She was not sure if Vijay could handle this shock anymore. The way he described his love for his daughter made Dr. Priti shiver and left him with a cold feeling. But Dr. Priti popped the question, "So what happened that night?"

Vijay started describing, "One night I was working late in the office, I had a few meetings and my mom called me. She seemed very scared. The mother said that her uncle is quite unwell and has been hospitalized. I immediately left the office at that moment and started traveling home. After reaching home, I told my mother, Priti, and Anamika to pack their bags as this was going to be a long journey. We were ready to leave and I started driving. It was raining that night.

So I was driving slowly, but it was a highway. There were no lights on the road, nothing was visible. I was only able to see the other car's headlights and nothing else. All those heavy vehicles were passing by. A truck was coming forward with a speed of 100 km/hr. I believed that truck was trying to overtake my car. I did not want to take any risk so I let it go. But one more truck came right in front of me out of nowhere. The truck must have crossed the speed of 120 km/hr and the driver of that truck looked too drunk. The truck got out of control and it hit my car straight. I tried to dodge but got hit by a rock and at last, the car overturned. Priti and I fell out of the car. My mother and my angel Anamika got stuck inside. We all were lying on the road and nobody thought to help us. I came to my senses after a while. So I got up and realized that I was covered in blood. I couldn't understand anything. What has happened? I asked myself. Then I got up and ran towards Priti. She was unconscious and covered in blood. I picked her up and saw that she was breathing. So I made her lie down in a broken hut on the corner of the highway.

Dr. Priti was listening to Vijay without even a flinch. Her heart was about to shatter with the other part that Vijay was going to describe.

Vijay continued, "Then I started searching for mom and Anamika. I saw that both of them were inside the car. I pulled out Anamika, and she passed out due to heavy blood loss. I could not hold my tears but I was determined to save their lives. I took mom and Anamika with me. Then kept both of them in the same hut. I made sure that all three of them were breathing. I tore my shirt and tied it on my mother's head."

He then wiped the blood off Priti's face. Vijay was strong enough and did not give up even in that situation. He was trying to stop the cars. The night was stormy, it was raining heavily, and not even a single car was ready to stop. He kept shouting, and screaming, "My family will die. Please stop the car. Please help me, I beg you."

But no one was kind enough to stop the car. Time was running out and he realized that if he did not bring them to the hospital, they would not survive.

Vijay had tears in his eyes and said, "I used to run and go to that hut, check their breath and then come running towards the highway, asking for help. My head was bursting with pain but nobody helped me."

Vijay started searching for his mobile. But it was so dark and rainy that nothing was visible. He could not even find his wallet. He thought he could get help from people who live nearby. But there was no one. He could hear the sound of "Nothing". Fortunately, Vijay found one hand cart. It was quite big. He took that hand cart and reached near the hut. He started to pick up all his family members and put them in that hand cart. To avoid any further accidents he tied them all with the rope and started searching for help.

The nearest hospital was 4 kilometers away from the highway but he kept running, limping hard, and did not stop. He would only stop to look at their breath and then used to run again.

After running for half an hour, Vijay reached a petrol pump. He parked the cart under a tree and went inside to ask for help. He saw an old guy sitting at the petrol pump.

He was about to ask that old guy but then fell unconscious at that moment and then opened his after 3 months in Tarabai hospital.

Tears were rolling down Dr. Priti's cheeks when she heard the terrifying case of Vijay.

It was a nightmare of his life.

Vijay continued, "I don't know how long it won't let me sleep. Perhaps, the man at that petrol pump must have taken us to the hospital. It was such a horrible highway.

It had no facility, no electricity, and the worst part, no help around. Our government should construct some small clinics in such places. So that victims can be saved. Everyone is not as lucky as my family."

Dr. Priti sighed and started staring at Vijay. She was worried if this poor guy could survive without his family.

She said, "You are right, there should be facilities at such a place... anyways, it is midnight and you must be sleepy. Tomorrow you are getting discharged, it's going to be a long day Vijay. Good night."

Dr. Priti switched off the lights and gazed at Vijay while leaving. She saw the content look on his face and excitement in his eyes to meet his family.

She wanted to tell him the truth but felt helpless. She decided to keep quiet and left the room.

The next day, Vijay was discharged from the hospital. Vijay and his uncle were waiting outside the corridor, waiting for both doctors. They wanted to thank Dr. Priti and Dr. Shekhar for their efforts. Doctor Priti kept looking at Vijay. Vijay met Dr. Shekhar and thanked him.

Vijay greeted, "Good morning doctor. Thanks a lot. It wouldn't have been possible without you two. Today I am going to meet my family, only because of you."

He also thanked Dr. Priti. He said, "If time permits, we will meet again."

After this, Vijay and Deendayal Ji left for their home. Deendayal Ji got nervous on their way back home. He was worried when Vijay would come to know about the truth. He will be thunderstruck to hear the news.

There were hope and eagerness in Vijay's eyes to meet his family that threatened his uncle. When they reached home, his uncle stopped outside.

Vijay asked, "What happened? You don't want to come inside?

Deendayal Ji replied, "Vijay, I have something to say to you and it is very important."

Vijay was eager to meet his family and told Deendayal Ji that whatever he wanted to say, will be discussed inside the house. He could not hold his excitement and run towards the main door.

Vijay called out to everyone, "Mom…..Anamika….. Priti, I am home and see who is here."

As soon as Vijay opened the door, he saw the three pictures hanging from the wall with a garland of flowers. Anamika's mouth organ was lying on the floor right under her picture. Everything stopped in front of Vijay. All his senses went numb. Vijay slowly walked in and took the Mouthorgan. He kept looking at Anamika's picture and fell to his knees. He started crying like a child. He was yelling and screaming for hours. He could not believe his eyes. He was kissing that mouth organ again and again. He never felt so helpless in his entire life.

Deendayal Ji could not gather the courage to go inside and tell Vijay about everything. He was waiting at the main door with tears in his eyes. He knew that if he went inside, he would be witnessing the most heart-wrenching thing. But he decided to face the situation.

Deendayal Ji sneaked into the house and saw that Vijay was lying on the floor, crying his eyes out. He ran towards Vijay and hugged him.

He wiped Vijay's tears, "Stop crying, my child". He was consoling Vijay but at the same time he started crying himself.

Vijay asked in a quivering voice, "Why? Why have I been kept in such a big deception till now? Why didn't you tell me?

Deendayal Ji apologized to Vijay and said that he was helpless at that time.

He confessed, "Please forgive me, Vijay, I was helpless. Your condition was very sensitive when you got out of the coma. The doctors suggested hiding the tragedy from you. I did it only for you, my child."

Deendayal Ji made him understand that he was so weak that if everything had been told at that time, he could have died of shock. Nobody was ready to lose him, neither the doctors nor his uncle.

He added, "Vijay, I am alone in this world. I have no one except you. I did what I thought was right at that time. It was an honest effort to save your life."

Vijay was still in shock, "What will I do now? God took away my angel Anamika, my wife…and my mother. For whom will I live now, for whom? I want to die today. I want to go to my Anamika. Yes, that is it, I will kill myself."

Vijay grabbed Anamika's picture and held it close to his chest.

Deendayal Ji told him, "No Vijay. You won't do any of these. Hey, look at me. Why don't you think that I had to burn my sister and the entire family? Have you burnt and buried your people? Vijay, I did it, I burnt that innocent child with these hands. I couldn't sleep for two weeks after that. Can you imagine what must have happened to my soul at that time? I have done everything without uttering a word. I have done it. At this age, I had to burn the bodies of my children.

I was getting punished for nothing. My hands were trembling at that time, my heart was bursting with pain when I burnt that little girl. And now you are going to leave me too. I cannot keep watching my children die. I beg you, Vijay, I beg you. If you try to do anything like this then I will give up my life before you."

Vijay wiped his tears, "but tell me now who else is left for me in this world? My love Priti, she was my source of happiness, my everything. How will I survive without her? All I am left with are her memories in this house. Now those memories will haunt me every minute, every second of my life."

Deendayal Ji asked him, "Promise me…that you will never even think of committing suicide."

Vijay nodded and continued to stare at Anamika's picture. But Vijay never got out of that shock.

Every time he used to see Anamika's face in the mirror, sometimes he felt his mother was standing at the door and sometimes he used to hear Priti's voice. Vijay was hallucinating all the time.

He used to sit with Deendayal Ji for dinner but then he used to get up without eating anything.

He was not able to sleep the whole night. He used to sit on the chair all night and fall asleep there. His overthinking started giving him major health issues. One day Deendayal Ji noticed that his ears were bleeding. Deendayal Ji used to call doctors every time. He took care of Vijay as much as he could.

Deendayal Ji was trying everything to make Vijay feel alive. But he was lost in the memories of his beloved wife, and his loving daughter. Sometimes he used to take sleeping pills to close his eyes.

Vijay used to complain that even after taking pills, he could not sleep. His head used to burst with pain. After a few days, he had trouble breathing.

To stay away from this sorrow, Vijay started drinking alcohol. He was not conscious half of the time and started losing weight.

It was 23rd October, Anamika's birthday. Vijay kept his bottle aside and went out to buy a cake. He got the cake and went to the graveyard. He kept the cake, candles, and balloons on Anamika's grave. He started celebrating her birthday while wiping his tears.

He tied the balloon to the grave and he sat down. Vijay started talking to his angel in the graveyard. He had a little grown beard, gray pants, and old shoes.

Vijay murmured. "Anamika, my angel, look at me baby, today is your birthday, I used to forget otherwise but I got you some cake and balloons. Don't you like balloons? Then try these chocolates. Okay, let's cut the cake. You turned seven today. Happy birthday my child."

Tears started rolling down his cheeks while wishing her a birthday. Vijay made three pieces of cake and put them on the grave.

Vijay was still talking to her, "Eat this cake and the other one is for your grandma and this one for your mother. I will not eat anything, I am very angry with you guys. You all have left me alone. Look, I've got your mouth organ too. Look how I play."

Vijay started playing the tune and then fell asleep on the grave. Deendayal Ji was looking for him the whole night. He finally saw Vijay lying his head down on Anamika's grave. He could not stop crying after seeing Vijay's condition.

Deendayal Ji screamed at the top of his lungs, "God, why are you making this child suffer so much? You are punishing him for what? Why are you punishing him?"

He picked up Vijay and carried him home. He could not see Vijay's drowning condition.

He insisted Vijay stop drinking, "You will die if you continue to drink day and night, you don't even recognize people these days. Vijay, you will destroy your remaining life. Please do not do this. Please stop drinking."

But Vijay did not listen to anything. The next day Vijay woke up in the morning and started drinking alcohol as usual. Deendayal Ji saw his behavior and tried to stop him again.

Vijay got angry, "You know what uncle, I am alive because of alcohol, Otherwise I would have gone by now. You cannot stop me from drinking. This bottle has kept me alive through these years. I keep thinking about Anamika. How can I forget my daughter? How can I forget the love of my life? It hurts so much, uncle. I do not have words to describe this pain. I wish I too had died in that accident. I wish….please help to forget this. Help me."

Deendayal Ji kept quiet for a while. He told him that he can't live his life in this way.

Vijay had not eaten anything for the past four days.

He consoled Vijay, "Life and death is the one fact, my child. What was meant to happen has happened. None of your family members would be happy to see you like this from heaven, wouldn't they?"

Deendayal Ji suggested to him that Vijay should get back to his office. At least he would forget the pain while being busy at work. He believed that if Vijay got engaged in work, then slowly he might forget everything. After all, his mother had a lot of expectations. She always used to pray for Vijay's better future and long life.

Vijay could not feel anything at that moment. All he saw was his mother's face in front of his eyes. He started crying again and kept staring at the floor. Along with tears, blood started running down from his ears and nose. Deendayal Ji got scared after watching his condition.

Deendayal Ji shouted, "Vijay you are bleeding. Get up. Let's go to the doctor."

Vijay was numb. He was sitting on that floor and did not move. Deendayal Ji got scared to death. He did not want to lose Vijay. He took Vijay to the nearby physician and told the doctor about his past experiences. Vijay started drinking in that clinic too. The doctor realized that Vijay had not changed his clothes for many days as he was stinking like a rotten potato. The doctor told Deendayal Ji to change Vijay's clothes as he was too drunk to understand anything.

A few doctors came and checked Vijay's heartbeat. After an hour of examination, they told Deendayal Ji, "See Mr. Deendayal, Vijay's mind is getting affected due to extreme anxiety and the body is getting weak. The body is not getting any nutrition."

Deendayal Ji sadly looked at the doctor and told him that he was helpless. He could not stop Vijay from drinking.

The doctor suggested to Deendayal Ji to take him out of that house. The memories of his family were haunting Vijay and that was the only reason he was taking more time to heal.

"If he continued to stay in that house, he might never cope up," said the doctor.

There was a high chance of having a brain tumor in his case. The doctors also suggested the option of remarriage. But Deendayal Ji knew that Vijay loved Priti more than his life and he would never agree to marry anyone else.

But then he decided to take Vijay to their native place. Vijay's ability to think and understand was almost negligible. The next day Deendayal Ji and Vijay left the house. The family had a beautiful house in the village. Deendayal Ji was confident that this change would help Vijay and that he could start a new life. They lived in that village for almost a year. Vijay was still hallucinating and drinking all the time.

On the death anniversary, Vijay again returned to that Shahpur highway. This time he was carrying a bottle of liquor and some flowers in another hand.

Vijay kept those flowers on the site of the accident and started staring at that road. He started getting uneasy after having a flashback of that entire nightmare.

He immediately got up and sat near his car. He opened his bottle and started drinking while wiping his tears.

Then he heard the sound of a car colliding there. He started running towards the car.

A woman and a little girl were covered in blood. Vijay realized that they were alive and he suddenly started laughing. He laughed harder as tears rolled down his eyes.

Vijay continued to laugh, "Hahahaha. This highway took two more lives."

Then he went quiet and sat near the wounded girl. That girl reminded him of Anamika.

He realized what could happen to that innocent child if he continued sitting there.

Vijay started blabbering, "No. She can't die. I will save this child. I will save everyone. Nobody should die."

He tried to stop cars and trucks. Nobody was ready to help him this time as well.

A few people stopped their car but ran away as they saw the accident. Vijay was getting angry as there was nobody to help them.

Vijay tried to fix their car but did not succeed. He lifted that woman on his shoulder and carried the child in his arms. He started running towards the hospital. People on that highway continued to watch this in silence. But nobody helped them.

He was determined to save their lives. He continued to run without taking any breaks.

Vijay reached the hospital's corridor and met Dr. Priti. She noticed that Vijay was carrying two people. She ran towards him to ask what was happening. She asked him what the case was.

Vijay told her about the incident and begged her to save their lives.

Doctor Shekhar came out of the room hearing this. He rushed towards the victims and called ward boys, "Ward boy, get the stretcher. Take them to the operation theatre."

A few minutes later Dr. Shekhar recognized Vijay. He asked Vijay who these people were.

Vijay replied, "Don't know! They had an accident on the highway. I have brought them."

After saying this, Vijay fell asleep on the hospital bench while drinking his liquor. He did not recognize anyone at that time since he was too drunk.

The next day ward boy and Dr. Priti came, and they woke up Vijay. He opened his eyes and saw Dr. Priti standing in front of him.

Vijay recognized Dr. Priti that morning. He smiled and said, "O I told you we will meet again."

But then he took his liquor bottle and started drinking again.

Dr. Priti brought good news to Vijay. The people he brought to the hospital had come to their senses.

Dr. Shekhar told Vijay, "Do you know who the lady and that girl whom you saved yesterday?"

Vijay was drinking and had no idea what Dr. Shekhar was talking about. He was happy that he saved their lives.

Dr. Shekhar gladly replied, "It is a huge deal, Mr. Vijay, they are our Mayor's….Ramesh Joshi's wife and daughter."

Mayor was sitting in the same room with Dr. Shekhar. Mayor went to thank Vijay for his kindness Mayor said with folded hands, "I don't have words to thank you enough. If I could be of some use to you, I would consider myself lucky."

Vijay acknowledged with a teary eye, "You are very lucky sir that someone was there to help.

But that night I wasn't so lucky. Please do not cry. You should be happy that your soul is not ruined….like me. That night my whole life was destroyed. Anyway, I am leaving. But before I go, I want to meet that girl. Please allow me"

Dr. Shekhar told Priti to show him the little girl's room.

Vijay went inside her room. He saw that both mother and daughter were kept in the same room. The child's mother was lying down and thanked Vijay with folded hands. The little girl smiled at Vijay. Soon the mayor also came there.

Vijay smiled and told the mayor, "Look at that girl, today I am happier than you as a father.

I felt accomplished by saving her life. Because she gave me a purpose to live today.

For one year I have been wandering for my peace of mind. And today my mind has got peace."

Vijay took some colors and liquor with him while leaving the hospital. He went to the accident site.

Vijay opened the door of his accidental car and wrote DRIVE SLOWLY on it. He also wrote SAVE YOUR FAMILY at the bottom so that people would notice this sign. He then hung the sign on the tree.

He then hung the door around his neck, with a big stick in one hand and a bottle of wine in the other. He stood on the highway day and night.

Every day he used to hold this board in his hands and kept shouting by showing it towards trucks and cars. Some people used to laugh at him and some called him a psychopath.

Every week he wrote different messages like "DO NOT DRINK AND DRIVE" or "SAVE YOUR FAMILY". Day and night, he was standing on the corner of the highway with a lantern

In his hand. In the scorching sun, he used to tie his shirt on his head, and in heavy rain, he used to wrap plastic around his body. But he stayed on that highway with his signboards.

Vijay kept a hand cart with him which can be used to save victims. It was the same hand cart in which Vijay carried his family during his accident.

Vijay had built a small hut near the highway. People passing by that road used to wonder who this guy…was. Why was he standing like this?

Some people started taking his pictures and some tried to interview him.

The news of saving the mayor's wife and the child was published in the newspaper.

One afternoon, Vijay was sitting under the tree playing the mouth organ. He could hear the cries of some people from afar. He got up and went behind the bush.

He saw that some robbers were trying to rob a family with a car. The robbers had big knives, and bicycles in their hands. Vijay sneaked up from behind and snatched the knife from the robber.

Vijay warned the robbers, "Come on, stand in a corner, and leave the girl." He told the family to go and sit in that car. He was ready to deal with the robbers. He had nothing to lose after all.

The robbers saw that Vijay was talking to the family and suddenly tried to snatch the knife back.

Vijay quickly grabbed the knife in the other hand and attacked the robber's knee. The other robber tried to choke Vijay but Vijay hit a hard kick in his chest. The first robber struck Vijay with the chain but Vijay used a knife in his hand to stop the robber. The robber's t-shirt was torn and he started bleeding. They got scared and ran away from Vijay.

Vijay then went outside his small hut and tied a bandage on his hand.

Vijay looked at his hand and whispered, "Don't know when these red colors will leave me."

Vijay was hungry, so he got his drink in one hand and hit the door of Dhaba in the nearby villages. Makhan Singh, the owner of that Dhaba, was a jovial person. Vijay was sitting at the Dhaba. Makhan Singh could not recognize him. He had a feeling that he had seen Vijay around the area. But he remained quiet and served him food.

The next day Vijay again went to Makhan Singh's Dhaba. He was sitting at his usual place and started playing the mouth organ. This time Makhan Singh could not control it. He decided to talk to him.

Makhan Singh asked him, "Are you that guy who stands on highways and saves people?

I saw you at my Dhaba every day. But how did you end up in this situation brother? Don't you get scared while standing on that highway? You are doing a great job, we all are proud of you"

Vijay angrily replied. "Why are you asking me all this? Don't you know that people around here call me crazy…they have declared me as a psychopath."

Makhan Singh knew something wrong had happened with Vijay.

He consoled Vijay, "I know my friend. I read in the newspaper that you had lost your family on this highway. I have also lost some of my loved ones here. Let me know if you need any help. I am already here to help you. You can call me anytime."

Vijay smiled and said, "Sure brother, I need people like you to save others' lives. Can you please bring me some food? I haven't eaten anything for the last two days. This bottle helps me to forget about my family but my stomach reminds me that I need to stay alive… stay alive to save others."

Every day in the newspapers there was an article written about Vijay. Vijay's uncle Deendayal Ji used to read these articles in the newspapers and he also used to visit him on the same highway.

Deendayal Ji used to watch Vijay standing on the side of the highway. Vijay was never able to see him as there were many vehicles on the road. He used to stand at the corner with his door on that highway. One day Vijay noticed Deendayal Ji and he started walking towards him.

Vijay told him with a content look on his face, "Uncle look at me. I finally got that peace I was looking for. Now don't stop me from fulfilling this mission of my life. I have accepted this Highway as a part of my life."

Deendayal Ji proudly said, "Hey son, I did not come here to stop you from this noble work but to support you. You left me in that house but I tried everything to save you from this grief.

But I am happy to know that you are working so hard and found your peace. You have no idea how proud I feel today. I will support you till my last breath"

Vijay was happy but also concerned about his uncle. He was not sure where he would live. His life, his house…. everything was that highway. I don't want you to sleep in the dust of the road here, so you go back home.

Deendayal Ji was determined to help Vijay. He said that it is better to die on this highway rather than live with the memories of the people whom we lost.

One night Deendayal Ji slept in Vijay's hut and Vijay was sleeping outside the hut.

Vijay kept remembering that horrible accident in his dream, and suddenly the sound of a car crash woke Vijay up. He panicked and at the same time, Deendayal Ji came out of his hut.

Vijay told him, "It seems that there has been an accident, let's go. You take the lantern and find out where the accident happened. I will come with a hand cart."

Deendayal Ji went and started searching for the car. It was dark on the highway.

Both of them reached the spot and saw that two boys were covered in blood.

They were still breathing and their bikes had fallen away.

Vijay called Deendayal Ji, "Uncle, they have lost a lot of blood, we have to take her to the hospital with water."

Vijay picked up both of them and put them on the hand cart. Both started running towards the hospital. It was very dark. Deendayal Ji was running ahead with a lantern and torch while Vijay was carrying them in a hand cart.

Finally, both of them reached the hospital.

Deendayal Ji called out to the doctors and told them that it was an emergency. Vijay started looking for Dr. Shekhar and Sr. Priti.

In this, Dr. Priti came out from a room and saw that Vijay was carrying the hand cart with two injured bodies.

Vijay pleaded with her, " Madam, these two boys have had an accident. A lot of blood has been shed. Please do something."

Dr. Priti started examining both the guys.

Dr. Priti realized they both were breathing. She immediately called the ward boys and told them to get a stretcher. She took them into the operation theater.

While putting the body on the stretcher, the wallet fell from the guy's trousers.

Vijay picked up the wallet and saw that he was a student.

Both kept waiting for the operation to get over and finally Dr. Priti came out of the operation theater.

Dr. Priti told them that she was able to save only one of them. The other guy had severe injuries and doctors could not save him.

Vijay's hand went straight into his pocket, he took out the bottle of liquor and started drinking.

Vijay started blaming himself, "All this happened because of me, I delayed in bringing him. I just hate myself."

Dr. Priti told him, "It was not your fault Vijay. Why are you blaming yourself? Vijay, you tried your best. The blame goes to those people who think of the highway as a playground. You are doing such wonderful work and I will help you in this, do not lose hope."

The next day the police called the family of both the students to the hospital. One student survived and the other one died. One family was thanking God and the other was cursing God.

Vijay and Deendayal Ji were heartbroken to watch the family's condition.

Vijay whispered to his uncle that the accident did not kill the boy, but it killed all his family members. Their hopes died. Due to one mistake, five people died that day.

Vijay kept telling Deendayal Ji that they had to find a faster way to reach the hospital.

They were not having enough money to have a vehicle or any car.

Deendayal Ji suggested to Vijay that they should take Dr. Priti's help in this situation and ask her if she could arrange a vehicle for us.

Vijay was reluctant to take Dr. Priti's help. He was not sure that anyone, especially a highly qualified doctor, would help an idiot like him.

But Deendayal Ji convinced him that she would definitely help and told him that Dr. Priti reminded him of Priti……his wife. Deendayal Ji could see in Dr. Priti's eyes that she had some strange affection towards Vijay.

Vijay was surprised to hear that. He avoided that topic and told him that they had to find another way to save people.

Vijay was thinking about saving people and helping the victims on the highway all the time. He suggested that they would take away to the woods.

The next day both Vijay and Deendayal Ji started a survey of the whole jungle area to find shortcuts and clear paths. They were marking the points which could lead to the easiest way of reaching the hospital.

Vijay called Deendayal Ji, "Come from here, maybe this road leads to the hospital… See, there was probably a way here before."

Deendayal Ji told Vijay that this was going to be very difficult.

He murmured, "There is such a dense forest, what will we do if an accident happens at night? At least we can see the vehicles move on the highway… something is visible. Here in this forest, we can't see anything at night."

Vijay was drunk that time as well and told Deendayal Ji that they could walk in the jungle in the same way they used to do on the highway. The only thing was they had to clean stones and debris there. They saw the same petrol pump at the end of that road. They walked for five more minutes and reached the hospital. Both of them had marked the road so that they would not forget it the next day.

Both Vijay and his uncle started working with an axe and spade to clean stones and create shortcuts.

One car halted on the highway and Dr. Priti came out of the car. Vijay was standing on the highway as usual….. with a signboard hanging around his neck.

Dr. Priti was dressed like a queen, wearing a gorgeous saree, a nice gajra on her hair, and had a thali for puja in her hands. She kept coming close to Vijay. He couldn't recognize her as she was always wearing her uniform.

Vijay finally realized it was Dr. Priti as she came in front of him. He could not take his eyes off her. He kept staring at her for a while. He had flashbacks of his wife…..their first fight….their date nights….and the day they got married.

Dr. Priti asked Vijay, "What happened? Am I looking weird?" I had no time to get ready so I wore whatever was handy."

Vijay nervously replied, "No…actually… I have never seen you in a saree. That is why I could not recognize you. Anyway, thankfully there was no accident today. If I need any help, I will come to the hospital."

Dr. Priti smiled, "Do you always think about death, accidents, and highways?"

Vijay told her, "I thought you were here to help me. Is there anything special today?"

She wanted to help him a lot, and when the time came, she was going to prove it too. She met Vijay that day because it was her birthday. She used to visit the temple every year on her birthday.

She thought she could ask Vijay to join her.

Vijay wished her and refused to go with Dr. Priti inside the temple.

Dr. Priti was also stubborn. She kept asking him and at last Vijay agreed to go with her. But he said that he would stand outside.

Vijay looked at Dr. Priti while walking thinking there might be no future for them. He was an addict and she was a qualified doctor. He wanted to say a lot of things but he chose to stay quiet that day.

They had a good talk while walking. She apologized to Vijay for not telling him the truth when he was in the hospital. Vijay smiled and did not say anything. They shared their interest, their taste in music, and many things. Both kept talking and reached the temple. Vijay remained standing outside and Dr. Priti went inside.

Dr. Priti prayed for Vijay that day. She wanted to have a good life. She also realized that she was madly in love with Vijay.

Both of them returned with some mixed feelings. None of them was sure about the next steps. They said goodbye to each other and Dr. Priti went home.

The next day Vijay and Deendayal Ji started working in the forest to make a shortcut as they decided. So they started removing stones and blocks from their way and Vijay was putting an arrow mark showing the direction of the way to the hospital.

Vijay heard a loud crash. Both ran towards the spot and saw that one car had fallen from the mountain into a ditch.

Deendayal Ji shouted, "Vijay That car has fallen in the ditch."

Vijay went down to the ditch and told his uncle to get that hand cart.

Deendayal ran towards the hut and got the hand cart. Vijay went down from the plateau and checked the car. He saw that the driver's body was lying in that car and he was not breathing either.

Vijay looked around for other members and found a foreign lady. When Vijay checked the foreigner girl, she opened her eyes slowly and went unconscious.

Deendayal Ji reached the top of that plateau with a hand cart. But he could not get down at the spot where Vijay was standing.

Vijay decided not to waste any time and started running towards the hospital. He carried that girl in his arms and rushed towards his destination.

Vijay screamed, "Doctor, doctor Priti…Doctor Shekhar it's an emergency……help……."

Dr. Priti came out from one ward and checked the girl. She and the other staff took the girl into the operation theater.

Soon the police arrived at the hospital to investigate the case. Police inspector Sawant and his team of four constables started asking questions to Deendayal Ji about an accident of a foreign girl. Police did a thorough investigation and found their bags. They were lucky enough to find the ID proof along with some other documents.

Inspector Sawant asked Deendayal Ji, "Who are you and how did you bring this foreign girl from there, how did the accident happen? Have you not killed that girl for money? Where is your gang? You people have committed murder, I will not leave you this time."

Deendayal Ji replied, "Please inspector, we have not murdered anyone. My nephew and I are trying to save lives on the highway. That is our daily work.

That girl's car fell from the hill. We picked up that girl and brought her here. Her driver had died at the same place. We brought her to the hospital to save her life and you are blaming us."

Inspector Sawant angrily said, "Don't lie to me, there have been cases of looting on the highway."

Vijay came out from the hospital and intervened in the investigation.

Vijay angrily said to the inspector, "That ain't no street garbage, you keep calling it old man. I am his nephew Vijay and I picked up that foreign girl. You can ask me whatever you want. I am ready to answer any question."

Inspector Sawant brashly asked him, "Aren't you the guy who saved the mayor's wife? It seems that the whole family is engaged in this work, uncle is good…….but if the government is not so concerned about this work then why are you taking so much interest?"

Vijay took his small alcohol bottle and started drinking.

Vijay told that inspector, "I have nothing to do with the government. That highway took away everything from me."

Inspector Sawant curiously asked, "Why? What happened to you?"

Vijay avoided the topic of his family and asked if they could leave. Inspector Sawant told him that they had to come back once the girl came to her senses. They also asked Vijay's address and wanted to track his location.

Vijay started laughing.

Inspector Sawant wondered why he would be laughing at this situation. Vijay told them that he did not have any address or permanent home and left the hospital.

Deendayal Ji was sitting outside the hut and reading the newspaper, Vijay was standing on the highway with a signboard hanging on his neck like every day.

While reading the newspaper Deendayal Ji saw the picture of that same foreign girl they had saved last night.

Deendayal Ji called Vijay and both of them started reading about the girl. It was written that the girl was out of danger. Police got to know that she was a European and came to India from England.

She was a journalist and came to India to document the life of Indian farmers.

Vijay was happy that they were able to save her life. But after that incident, Vijay became very famous. All the news channels including English, Hindi, and Marathi platforms started visiting the highway to interview Vijay.

One day a reporter asked Vijay why he chose such a difficult job and devoted his whole life to it.

Vijay replied, "This highway has taken a lot of things from me, That's why I have taken this responsibility, I have nothing to do with the government."

Journalist asked him again if he would like to get some help from the government. But Vijay rejected the offer with conviction.

The journalist said, "Sir, you saved the life of Miss Katie Ball, Mayor's family. People are talking a lot about you. What do you want to say?"

Vijay smiled and said, "It is a life after all. Pain remains the same for all. Even if I saved a beggar's life I would have felt the same as I felt after saving those two lives. I have learned this by losing my loved ones."

After this interview, all the news channels started looking for Vijay. They were taking interviews with people staying near the highway.

Three days later, Katie Ball came to her senses. She was fully covered and left with a small bandage on her hand.

Dr. Priti greeted her, "Hello Katie, how are you feeling? I am Dr. Priti."

Katie Ball was confused. She asked Dr. Priti, "Where am I? What happened to my car? I don't remember anything."

Dr. Priti told her that she had an accident on the highway but now she was out of danger.

Katie Ball asked about her driver but Dr. Priti apologized. She told Katie that he lost his life and by god grace, you were brought here by highway life vigilante on time. Only because the doctors were able to save your life.

Katie was sad but Dr. Priti made her feel comfortable. She ordered some ice cream for Katie and told her to take some rest. Katie thanked her for her care and kindness. She asked Dr. Priti to let her meet the vigilante once. Dr. Priti smiled and nodded, "Sure Katie but first you take some rest. I will introduce you to the kindest man who saved your life."

The next day Vijay was drinking at Makhan Singh's Dhaba. Suddenly a car arrived and Dr. Priti got out with her friends.

Dr. Priti was wearing a knee-length dress and looking gorgeous as always. Vijay's eyes got stuck on her smile.

Dr. Priti saw Vijay and ran towards him. Vijay saw Dr. Priti coming towards him, he turned his face and hid the bottle.

Dr. Priti told him that she was there with her college friends. Vijay offered her to sit with him and asked her what she would like to eat.

Makhan Singh suddenly asked, "So Dr. Priti, what will you have today?"

Priti was shocked as she had never been to that Dhaba. But Makhan Singh told her not to worry, he knew her name because Vijay kept talking about her.

Dr. Priti blushed and asked, "What does he say about me?"

Vijay in despair, "I don't speak anything bad about you, some people are worthy of discussion, everyone is forced to praise them, you belong to those people, Priti."

Dr. Priti smiled and told him that he was a kind man. She has never met anyone like him to date.

After they finished dinner Vijay said goodbye and went outside. Dr. Priti tried to stop him but he left. Vijay had a fear that he might lose one more precious person from his life. His heart was not ready to get one more scratch so he tried to distance himself from Dr. Priti.

The next day Katie ball recovered and doctors decided to get her discharged from the hospital. Katie met Dr. Priti to thank her again.

Katie appreciated her efforts, "Thank you, Dr. Priti for doing so much for me, now I got a friend in India. I will never forget these days spent here with you. Thanks again."

Dr. Priti replied, "No, Katie it was my job to save your life. You are a guest of our country and it was my duty towards you. But you have got a friend in India. You can call me anytime."

Katie asked her, "Priti before leaving India, I want to meet that vigilante who has saved my life. I want to know more about this man who is doing such great work."

Dr. Priti told Katie, "Katie, you must meet him. He is a man of his word, he lost everything on that highway and became a mad vigilante. He is the person who went against all odds.....against all systems to save innocent lives on that highway."

Katie could see the spark in Dr. Priti's eyes for him and could not wait to see Vijay.

Katie was discharged from the hospital and went to meet Vijay the same day. Vijay was standing on the highway with a signboard hanging around his neck and wrote "ITS RAINING DRIVE SLOWLY, SAVE YOUR FAMILY". Vijay saw a foreign girl with an umbrella watching him from the other side of the road. Vijay didn't pay any attention and kept standing on the road, but suddenly Vijay saw that girl coming towards him. Vijay removed the signboard from his neck and took out his alcohol bottle from his pocket. He started drinking and picked up a shovel.

It was raining heavily that day. Vijay started walking towards the forest with a shovel. Katie started chasing him and followed him towards the forest.

Vijay sensed that someone was chasing him. He turned back and saw that it was Katie.

He asked her, "Do I know you?"

Katie smiled, "Yes you do."

Vijay remembered that he had seen her before somewhere.

He asked Katie, "Are you the same girl whom we took to the hospital two weeks ago? Am I right? But why are you here?.....it's raining."

Katie told Vijay that Dr. Priti has given her the idea about his work. She said that she has never met such a selfless life vigilante. Katie was mesmerized to know that he has given his life to save people on that highway and devoted himself to mankind. She thanked him for saving her life.

Vijay told her, "It has become my destiny now. I would have saved your driver too. But he was dead on the spot and we lost him.

Katie said, "You tried your best."

Vijay continued to tell her that it is a challenge that he has given himself… A sort of competition between the highway and his efforts. How much it could kill and how much could save. Each life was very important for him. He would fight to do this till his last breath.

Katie Ball asked him, "But why are you doing this?"

Vijay told her about his family and the horrible night incident on that highway. Katie was shaking and started crying after a while.

Vijay saw her crying and thought it was too much for her to handle.

He started avoiding her and continued walking towards the dense forest.

Katie stopped him, "Wait, Vijay, is there anything that I can do for you? Any contribution to this will be the greatest achievement of my life.

Vijay refused to take any help from her. He was determined to save all lives on his own. He left from there and went deep into the forest.

Katie wanted to help him at any cost. She decided that she will study Vijay's work and started preparing a document of that. She stayed there in a hotel for a few days to study Vijay and his work, she kept an eye on Vijay... what he does... how he works, every day Katie used to stand and report his activities. She decided to write about Vijay in the newspaper and also a book on him and his work.

Katie also decided that Vijay should get a Nobel prize for such purposeful work. A few days later She was leaving for London. Dr. Priti met to say goodbye at the airport.

Katie told Dr. Priti that she will be recommending Vijay's name for the Nobel Peace Prize.

Dr. Priti was shocked and asked her, "What are you saying? For Nobel? What do you think? Will they consider him for such an honor?

Katie asked, "Why don't you think so?"

Dr. Priti said, "Yes, I do. I think he is doing a great job. I am ready to give my life to him. But the Nobel is something different. But I guess Vijay doesn't believe in such things…I mean any prizes or awards…I doubt he might not like it because he is not ready to take any help from anybody."

Katie smiled, "That's why I have called you here Priti. If it all goes well you have to make him understand that it is for Vijay's good. It is up to you, but you have to convince him and you have to get him to England. I will bear all expenses. I got to go now but I will be in touch with you. Bye."

Dr. Priti and Katie hugged each other. Katie went back to London with a lot of hope for Vijay.

A few days later, Vijay was sitting at the Dhaba. He was completely drunk and fell asleep. One of the waiters came running and told Makhan Singh that some robbers had hijacked the whole public bus and gone to the forest. Vijay suddenly woke up and saw that everyone was panicking.

Makhan Singh told Vijay about the whole incident.

Makhan Singh said, "One of our waiters saw that some robbers were robbing a bus on the highway and when Deendayal Ji tried to enter the middle, they tied him to a tree and started beating him. We have to go fast and do something."

Vijay got angry after hearing this. He asked Makhan Singh and his waiter to grab some chilli powder. All three of them started running and reached the spot. They were hiding in the bush and looking for Deendayal Ji.

Vijay noticed from a distance that Deendayal Ji was tied to a tree and his nose was bleeding. He saw that the robbers had removed his pants and all of their faces were covered with black masks. They were continuously beating Deendayal Ji.

There were some other passengers on that bus as well. Everyone kept quiet out of fear.

But one of the passengers raised his voice, "Please leave that old man or else he will die. For god's sake leave him."

One of the robbers got pissed and slapped that passenger. The poor passenger started bleeding and shouting. Vijay attacked one of the members of that gang and hit him on the neck. He went unconscious… Vijay slowly moved forward and hid behind the bus. He saw that their leader was beating that passenger badly.

Vijay hit one robber on his back and that robber fell. Then he grabbed the leader and took his knife.

Vijay warned him by putting the knife on his neck. The leader told him that he would face the consequences if he tried to hurt him.

Vijay shouted, "Whatever you have done to my uncle, I will do the same with you. Be ready."

Vijay then threw that knife towards the tree and turned that leader around. He kicked on his crotch…the leader bent down. Vijay then grabbed his neck.

Other gang members tried to hold Vijay but Makhan Singh and his waiter attacked both of them from behind.

Vijay dragged the leader towards the tree. Meanwhile, Makhan Singh untied Deendayal Ji's rope and released him.

They gave that rope to Vijay and took Deendayal Ji to the hospital.

Vijay tied that leader with a tree and passengers helped him to deal with other gang members. They gained confidence after Vijay came to the rescue.

All passengers thanked Vijay for his great help and went towards the bus. Vijay punched that leader and put a red chilli powder in his eyes. The leader started yelling and shouting. Vijay escaped from that forest and ran towards the hospital.

7 March 2022

Vijay came running to the hospital and entered a ward where Deendayal Ji was kept. He saw his uncle lying on the bed with a bandage on his head. Dr. Priti was standing next to him.

She saw Vijay and came outside to talk to Vijay.

Dr. Priti told him that she had given some injections but his uncle had a deep stock. She asked Vijay how all that happened.

Vijay told her to sit on the hospital bench and both of them started talking.

Vijay briefed her, "Some robbers had hijacked a bus on the highway.

My uncle tried to intervene and they did this to him. I have also fed them those chillies that they will never forget."

Dr. Priti was worried, "But how long will this last Vijay, look at the age of your uncle, how long will he be able to support you like this, and you have to think about him."

Vijay gasped and replied, "Yes, I will not allow him to stay with me here and will send him back home. I can't put him at risk anymore. I have no one in this world except this kind man."

Dr. Priti looked at the floor and told Vijay, "I know you never considered me as a part of your life, but I gave you my heart a long time ago. I am telling this to you today with great courage. I don't know when it happened... How it happened but I love you more than anything."

Vijay got nervous and looked at Dr. Priti. He stood up and tried to leave the place. Dr. Priti stopped him.

She grabbed his hand and said, "Wait, Vijay, today you have to answer this question, what is the matter, what is lacking in me? I want to share your sorrow.... your grief. I can't see you suffering all the time."

Vijay replied with tears in his eyes, "You are not lacking anything, Priti... but I don't deserve you.

People marry someone to become life partners for eternity... to get the happiness of life... to get love... not to make their lives miserable. I don't deserve anybody.

I have nothing left in my heart... I cannot give you anything, which is why I stayed away from you all the time. Never let this dark shadow of my life enter your life too."

Dr. Priti started crying and asked him, "Tell me the truth, have you ever seen your wife Priti in me? Take a look inside your heart and speak. I kept my love in my heart for so long, I was afraid that I might lose you."

Vijay screamed at her, "Yes....yes I saw my wife whenever I met you. But what is the use of thinking about the glorious night when you know that there is no sunshine left in your life?

Why the hell do you want to marry me? Hey, I have become the dust of this highway that has nowhere to go. My life has no existence Priti... I am left with only pain and grief that might never go."

Dr. Priti told him while he was leaving that she loved him from the bottom of her heart and she could never forget him during the last breath. Even if he rejected her, she would continue to love him and always will. She asked him if they still could be friends.

Vijay nodded and ran away from the hospital.

The next day Deendayal Ji was discharged from the hospital. Vijay brought him to the hut and told him vividly, "Uncle, now you have to go back home. I cannot give you more trouble. Enough is enough."

Deendayal Ji pleaded with him, "Please let me stay here with you. I have already lost my family, my child, I don't want to lose you."

Vijay replied with a lot of anger, "Mamaji, why don't you understand that there is a danger to life here, every time destiny will not be so kind to you as it was the other day. What do you think, those robbers will sit silently like this? They will attack again… they will hurt you and I cannot see that. Please go back home…I beg you."

Deendayal Ji denied it and told him, "I understand Vijay, I have full faith in you. Nobody can harm me while you are here. Now we have Makhan Singh with us and Dr. Priti as well. Vijay, I got to know something about you and Dr. Priti. Vijay, you did not do the right thing by hurting her, she truly loves you… she will always do. I can see that in her eyes, can't you?"

Vijay got pissed and told him that she shouldn't have said this. He called her childish and thought she had gone blind in love… she had no idea what her future would look like.

He asked Deendayal Ji, "Would you allow your daughter to marry some crazy guy like me?

She would cry for the rest of her life if we got married. Anyways, all these things don't matter on the path I'm walking on."

Deendayal Ji tried to convince Vijay but he refused to listen to anything. He told him that he only wanted to fulfill his purpose and save the lives of innocent people.

While they were talking, Dr. Priti reached the highway.

Vijay was surprised, "What are you doing here?

Dr. Priti told him that she was there to meet Deendayal Ji. She wanted to check on him and gave him some medicine. But Dr. Priti left a letter and a book which was written by Katie. She told Deendayal Ji to read it. She left without talking to Vijay.

But Vijay saw that letter and also the book which was surprisingly written about him. The book mentioned his contribution towards society and also that his name was nominated for the Nobel Peace award.

Vijay could not believe his eyes. He read it twice but then he realized that those things didn't really matter to him.

He told Deendayal Ji to write that they do not need these things and did not want any help either.

Vijay removed the signboard and ran towards Dr. Priti. He gave that book and letter back to her. But Deendayal Ji got up to stop him.

Dr. Priti made him understand that if he got the Nobel Award then he can build a hospital on the highway using that money.

Deendayal Ji also jumped into that conversation, "She is right Vijay. Think about that day when a hospital by the name of Anamika will be built on this highway. Every victim will be treated here.

And how many Anamikas' will be saved? Why don't you think that it will save millions of lives, Vijay?"

Vijay started crying, he started having flashbacks of that night. He sat on that highway and cried his eyes out. Both Deendayal Ji and Dr. Priti tried to pick him up.

Vijay agreed to send his name for the Nobel Peace Prize. Dr. Priti had a teary eye that finally Vijay had got a ray of hope in his life. She went home and immediately wrote to Katie that she could go ahead with Vijay's recommendation. Katie was also delighted by seeing her reply.

The next week Katie went to her office and recommended Vijay's name by writing a whole paper on his contribution to the Nobel committee of Norway.

The committee noticed that such a contribution was never done by anyone.

The committee then forwarded Vijay's name to the Norwegian parliament. The Norwegian parliament ordered an analysis of this case to the committee. They told the committee to conduct serious research on this man and his work towards society. The committee got these orders and it sent all their delicacies to India. They wanted to meet the Indian government and this man Vijay.

The news went viral all over the media and all over news channels, the newspapers and magazines tried to cover Vijay's story. People all over the world came to know about this vigilante.

Mayor Ramesh Joshi and the government gave a positive response to the Nobel committee's delicate. As per the report of the delicate the Norwegian parliament decided and shortlisted Vijay for the Nobel Peace Prize.

Katie arranged all the things and the two tickets to Norway for Vijay and Dr. Priti. Priti did not tell this to Vijay but kept everything with her.

A few days later Dr. Priti and Deendayal Ji came to meet Vijay. He was standing as usual with the signboard around his neck.

Deendayal told him, "Vijay these are your tickets to Norway. Now the time has come for my child. Step forward to fulfill your dream."

Vijay was wondering about tickets and who had sent those. Dr. Priti stepped ahead and told him that they were sent by Katie.

Vijay asked Deendayal Ji when they would need to go. Deendayal Ji told him that he would stay back in India and Dr. Priti will accompany him to Norway. Vijay was surprised and happy at the same time. Dr. Priti looked at Vijay and told him to pack his bags.

A week late both Vijay and Dr. Priti arrived at Mumbai International airport. Deendayal Ji and Makhan Singh went with them to see off.

Deendayal Ji started crying while saying, "Take care of yourself, dear, and this lunatic as well."

Vijay laughed after a long time, "hahhahahaaa."

Both of them checked on security at the airport and they both left for Norway.

They were both sitting next to each other. Vijay apologized for his behavior to Dr. Priti. She smiled and told him that she was never angry or upset about his behavior.

Dr. Priti slept during the flight. While sleeping she tilted her neck on Vijay's shoulder. Vijay kept looking at her.

They both arrived at the Norway airport. Katie Ball came to the airport to receive them. Katie gave a hug to Dr. Priti.

They all greeted each other. Katie asked Dr. Priti, "Hey Priti, I know you were crying after Vijay rejected your proposal. Don't feel sad about it. He loves you too and trusts me that one day he will accept you."

Vijay was wearing the same dirty black jacket, black hard pants, and a beard with long hair.

They all went to the venue and Vijay finally received the Nobel award, medal, and prize money for his work.

It was declared in newspapers and all over the news channel that the Nobel Award was given to highway vigilantes. Vijay and Dr. Priti returned to India. As soon as they arrived at the airport in India, they saw a huge crowd waiting for them. They could see the security all around them.

Deendayal Ji and Makhan Singh came to the airport to receive them. Many people had gathered around Vijay including the minister, the mayor, and some members of parliament. He had made India proud and the government had thrown a big function in his honor.

People all around the nation, Civil officers, and social activists were invited to that function.

Vijay got an invitation so he and Deendayal Ji decided to attend it. It was 7 pm and the function was about to start. Vijay and his uncle sat with the government officials.

All the people around the country were invited to this function. Mayor Ramesh Joshi took the honor to speak at that function.

He started speaking, "Today I am going to tell you a reality which changed a person's life. 8 months ago today, my wife and child had an accident on the highway of Shahpur.

The blood of my body became cold, there was no ground under my feet, and I thought I lost everything in life. Can you imagine the person who has seen his entire family die in front of his eyes? What must have happened to him at that time…when his daughter was taking her last breath in front of him? He couldn't do anything, imagine how compelled that man would feel.

That's why I request every person who is driving on this highway or anyone else to drive with responsibility."

Mayor gazed at Vijay and saw his teary eyes.

He continued, "Life is not a joke. The people walking on the road should not be considered a worm or insects. Because one mistake will not only kill that man but his entire family."

"Today we are proud of this man who lost everything on that highway. But he did not lose his courage, his uncle Deendayal Ji, who is with us today gave courage and support to him.

He started the battle against the whole system, he never had any greed or any demands.

He took the responsibility of saving the lives of the people. I salute this man. He has not only made India proud but ensured our faith in humanity."

Vijay and Deendayal Ji started crying after they heard thousands of hands clapping for them. Vijay could not believe that someday he would receive such applause for his work. He determined that he would do his best to save more lives.

The function got over but people couldn't stop talking about Vijay. For the next 6 months, he got many reporters visiting his house, letters at doorsteps, and donations from celebrities.

After a year Vijay completed his dream. He finally built a hospital on that highway named "SAVITRI ANAMIKA HOSPITAL". It took exactly one year after Vijay won the Nobel Prize. But after receiving all the fame and money Vijay was the same. He was wearing the same black shirt, black jacket, and dirty pants. He had a beard and long hair.

Vijay decided to take a picture outside the newly built hospital with all his well-wishers. Makhan Singh, Deendayal Ji, and Dr. Priti posed in front of the hospital. Dr. Priti was standing next to Vijay. He finally held Dr. Priti's hand and looked at her. She looked at their hands held together and smiled with relief.

www.ingramcontent.com/pod-product-compliance
Lightning Source LLC
Chambersburg PA
CBHW022054150726
47990CB00003B/1085